THE LEGACY'S ORIGIN

ENCHANTED LEGACY
BOOK ONE

DAWN BROWER

USA TODAY
BESTSELLING AUTHOR
Dawn Brower
CAPTIVATING ROMANCES THAT TRANSCEND TIME

AUTHOR'S NOTE

Some stories do not have a happy ending. They rip you to shreds and you end it with the devastation of loss. This book will break your heart, so be prepared for desolation and despair. In the words of my editor: "Thanks for making me cry, ya meanie!"

The Enduring Legacy books tell the stories of the descendants of one family that were persecuted during the height of the witch trials in Scotland. This family is not real, and is the work of fiction, but what happens to them very much occurred to individuals in the sixteenth century and beyond.

While the story isn't one filled with joy, it is pivotal to understanding the rest of the books that are created, especially the first book by Amanda Mariel who took on the task of writing the twins from this book. I hope you find this compelling and continue on to the rest of the books in the series. There are several talented authors in this project and they will create some amazing stories for you all.

Sometimes bad things happen and you have no control over them. When you are going through a rough patch try to look for the silver lining and hope that in some way fate will restore the balance. No one ever said life would be easy, and for some it's one uphill battle after the next. This book is for everyone struggling with something. There is no joy to be found in it, and yet, we keep moving on. That perseverance and strength is what makes life bearable. Hold on to that and your steadfast determination will see you through anything.

ACKNOWLEDGMENTS

Many thanks to my cover artist, Victoria Miller—no mere words can express how much I appreciate you. You are fabulous as always. Also thanks to Elizabeth Evans—you make writing fun. Thank you for helping me and reading all my rough drafts.

Special thanks to all the authors in the Enduring Legacy project for working with me. It is nice to work with so many talented authors. Endeavors such as this one make writing that much more enjoyable and challenging. All of your hard work and dedication is appreciated.

CHAPTER 1

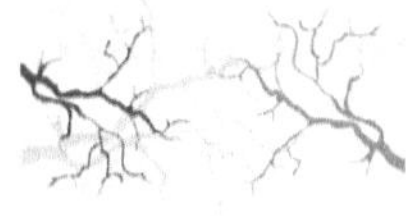

Scotland 1590

Sorcha Dalais Creag kept her son Lachlan at her side as they strolled along the field leading toward the cliffs of North Berwick. The rolling green dropped into a rocky expanse that led down to a sandy beach as waves in various shades of blue and white crashed the shoreline. She took in a deep breath, absorbing the fresh air and finding joy in the simple things in her life.

The sun highlighted Lachlan's red and gold locks, bringing out his hair's fiery hue. He'd inherited his coloring from her, and a part of her was rather glad for it. In some ways, it made him more hers, and while it might be selfish, she hoped he took after her in other ways as well. Her gifts gave her insight to people she'd not otherwise have and in turn, revealed the motivations of those around her. With that knowledge, she could help those who needed it most. Brian hated her need to offer assistance to those in dire straits. She loved her husband, but sometimes he didn't really understand her. Empathy was ingrained in her soul. She couldn't ignore it if she wanted to.

Brian was a good man and provided well for them. He was the fourth son of an earl, and without an inheritance to speak of. The little money he had, he'd used to open an all goods store They had a little bit of everything inside, and Sorcha took care of the apothecary side of their offerings. She gathered herbs and prepared them for sale each day. It gave her a purpose even when most people were afraid to be seen buying anything that might be associated with witchcraft.

Sorcha couldn't worry about such things. Deep inside, it hurt her not to help people. Feeling everything was part of her gift, and there was no escaping it. Everyone in her family had something special about them. Hers was to help others, and understanding their emotions was the first step in healing them inside and out. She'd take the risk of being termed a witch because the alternative made her stomach turn in distaste. To ignore an ailment could end in certain death, and she couldn't live with that possibility.

She stopped to pick some roseroot along the cliff's edge and put it in her apron pocket. The plant grew there and helped with certain illnesses. To be honest, she wasn't entirely sure how it worked, but sometimes, when certain wounds festered bright and red, the roseroot could be used to eradicate it.

Lachlan giggled and ran across the field behind her. She turned and shaded her eyes so she could see him better. The lad tripped over his feet and tumbled down a small hill. He sat up, shook his head, and then took off again.

"Och, lad," she said and then laughed. "Ye'll be the end of me yet."

There were no more herbs to be gathered, and it was time to head back in. She'd taken inventory the day before, and most of the herbs were fully stocked. Sorcha would only need a few things, and she could head into town later to add them to the store's coffers.

"Ma," he called out to her. "Catch me."

It was a game they often played, and she indulged him whenever possible. She chased after him as his laugher echoed on the wind. Lachlan ran as fast as his little legs would allow. He was a wee lad of five, and he'd been a happy bairn from day one. Sorcha lived a blessed life, and her son was her greatest joy. She'd do anything for him.

Sorcha lifted her skirts and ran faster. She

reached Lachlan and leaned down to scoop him into her arms. "There's a good lad," she said then kissed his cheeks. "It's time for a nap."

"No," he said pushing his lip out into a fine pout.

"Aye," she told him. "Little lads need proper rest tae grow into strong braw men." She cuddled him against her. His displeasure at the end of his fun washed over her. Lachlan's sadness became a part of her long enough for her to ease it. Soon, his smiles were wide on his face and his happy disposition shined through. "That's my lad. Are ye ready tae go now?"

He nodded. "Aye, Ma."

She carried him back to their seaside cottage. They didn't need much, and she saw to the house without help. She'd grown up with servants, as her father had been a great lord in the area. Their family had always been a part of the Dalais Barony. Her brother, Niall, was now the baron as their father had died a few years ago. She had one sister, Caitrìona, who was married to the town blacksmith. They probably could have set up finer matches, but finding love had been more important than status. Their family didn't do well without a strong emotion binding them together.

They neared the cottage, and Sorcha frowned when she noticed someone standing out front, pacing fretfully. As she got closer, she recognized the vicar, Tamhas Gall. He was tall, lanky, and had a nervous twitch. His brown hair was as equally dull as his muddy brown eyes. He twirled his hat in his hands as he waited for them to approach. Something about the vicar had always sat wrong with her, but she'd kept that to herself. He had a sweet wife who made up for his judgmental temperament.

"Good day," Sorcha greeted him. She set down Lachlan and asked, "How are ye?"

"I'm fine," the vicar said. "There's talk in the village ye have knowledge of medicine."

This was a fine line. She shouldn't openly admit an affinity to her skills with herbs. That alone could end her on trial for witchcraft. Most people didn't come right out and ask her. They didn't want to lose the one person able to help their ailments. The vicar; however, would have no problem turning her over to a witch hunter.

"Who's been telling tales about me?" she asked carefully.

"Please," he begged as he stepped forward. Anguish mixed with anxiety reverberated in that one word. "My lady wife is in her child bed. It's been hours, and I fear for her and the bairn."

Sorcha didn't need to hear any more than that. Beitris Gall needed her, and she'd do everything she could to save her. "I'll have tae take Lachlan tae Dalais Manor before I come see tae yer wife."

"We can drop him on the way," he said as he

gestured toward his nearby carriage. "Ye must hurry. I…"

"Say no more," Sorcha stopped him. "Ye may explain as we travel." She'd been gathering herbs all morning. Most of them wouldn't help her with Beitris's condition, but she didn't want to take the time to sort what she'd collected in her basket. It was easier to bring the entire lot of it with her and take out what she needed at the vicar's home.

Sorcha picked Lachlan up and placed him on the carriage seat, then joined him. The vicar didn't wait for her to say more and quickly hopped up as well. He grabbed the reins and snapped them to make the horses move. The carriage jolted forward, hitting every bump in the road on their way to Dalais Manor.

It was a short distance from Sorcha's cottage, so it didn't take them long to reach it. The stately manor had been in her family for generations, but was modest compared to most baron's homes. It didn't have a grand ballroom, but had a nice dining room. They could not have large parties, but they could have several dinner guests. The small library that doubled as Niall's study had been one of her favorite rooms. Her thirst for knowledge had grown by reading those limited supply of books. They didn't have a big family, and hadn't had to share sleeping quarters. They even had a couple extra bedchambers available for the occasional guest. It was still luxurious, just not obscenely so.

The carriage pulled to a stop in front of the manor. Sorcha stepped down and then reached up to grab Lachlan. "I'll be but a moment," she told the vicar and then headed inside.

Ailis, her brother's wife, greeted her as she entered. "Sorcha," she said, surprised. "We weren't expecting ye."

"It's the vicar's wife," she said. "The bairn is coming, and it's a difficult one. Will ye keep Lachlan while I see tae her care?"

Ailis nibbled on her bottom lip and rubbed on her protruding belly. She was expecting her first child with Niall. They were both anxious for their own bairn to come into the world in a handful of months. "Oh, dear," she said. "I do hope she's all right."

"She'll be fine, but I must go," Sorcha said. "Lachlan, be a good lad for yer auntie."

Lachlan hugged onto Sorcha's legs. "Go with Ma," he demanded.

Sorcha leaned down and kissed his chubby cheek. "It's nap time, and ye'll remember what I said about naps."

"Grow up strong," he said.

"That's my braw lad," she replied, ruffling his hair. "Auntie Ailis will take ye tae the nursery."

Ailis hugged Sorcha. "Do be careful," she whispered. "This might be too big of a risk."

Sorcha nodded. "I canna let her die." A part of her thought aiding of the vicar and his wife a foolish idea. The other side of her couldn't ignore the call to help others. She feared it would one day get her into a fine mess she couldn't find a way out of. All she could do was pray it never came, and this time would end as well as each one before. To selfishly allow Beitris and her babe to die in order to save herself—she'd never be able to live with that grief. So, she set aside those misgivings that plagued her and forged on. To her, there was no other choice she could make.

"Aye," Ailis agreed. "And I won't be talkin' ye out of it. Would be a waste of my breath, and it's difficult enough to force air in these days. The bairn is squeezing it out of me the bigger he gets."

Sorcha smiled. "They do that." Her family was growing with the addition of Niall and Ailis's bairn. Caitrìona had twin daughters, Sorcha had Lachlan, and soon a brand new bairn will join the mix. She couldn't wait to meet her new nephew. "I'll send word once I know more," she said and rushed out the door."

The vicar sat in the carriage where she'd left him. His agitation reverberated through the air, and she'd notice it even if she hadn't felt it first. He nearly squirmed in his seat and tapped the reins against his lap in a steady pattern. She stepped into the carriage and nodded at him. There were no words necessary. He flicked the reins and the horses started to move. The vicarage was near Dalais Manor on the north end of the estate. It was the duty of the barony to take care of the vicarage and pay for their living. The current vicar had taken over before her father had died. Niall had inherited the responsibility and hadn't liked it.

Her family believed in God and respected their religion, but had never been zealots. Tamhas Gall leaned heavy toward the side of witch hunting. He favored the king's command that all witches in Scotland be eradicated. Sorcha didn't believe in magic, but she did know there were special gifts given to certain people. Her family was a prime example of that. It wasn't magic though. Their gifts had been given to them by a higher power, and nothing bad came as a result of them. No one would ever convince her they were evil.

The carriage came to a halt outside the vicarage. Tamhas jumped down and tethered the reins to a nearby post, then showed her inside. Beitris's screams reverberated throughout. They became louder as they neared the bedroom. Sorcha stepped inside and sucked in a breath. Beitris had almost no color to her cheeks, and her skin was soaked in sweat. She panted heavily and didn't even notice when they entered.

"Beitris," Sorcha said softly. "How are ye?"

She turned her head to meet Sorcha's gaze. Her normally vibrant dark green eyes were now a dull shade that resembled a patch of dirty moss. She didn't talk, or even attempt to, as she continued to stare at Sorcha. Her head rolled back, and she collapsed into unconsciousness. "Och, this isna good at all."

Sorcha pulled the quilt back that covered Beitris's sweat-soaked body. It was worst than she feared. The sheets were stained red with blood, and chances of Beitris's survival went down every second that passed. The bairn might be saved though. If only she could wake her up.

"Beitris," Sorcha said as she tapped her cheek lightly. "Can ye open yer eyes?"

She moaned and slowly opened her lids. "Dinna think I can do this."

"I ken ye will," Sorcha replied. "If ye want the bairn tae live, ye must push the wee one out. Are ye ready?"

She shook her head. "I canna."

Sorcha checked to see if the bairn was ready to come. The head appeared to be stuck, so she eased it out a little to help Beitris. She was so close and hadn't even realized it. Why hadn't the vicar sent for a midwife or even Sorcha sooner? Had he really thought his wife could do this on her own? "Push the bairn out," Sorcha ordered.

Tears fell from Beitris's eyes, soaking her cheeks even more than they already were. "I canna," she insisted.

"Now," Sorcha told her. "Ye must or the bairn will be lost."

She didn't tell her that the bairn might still die or that her own life hung in the balance. First, the bairn had to be born into the world, and then the rest might be left to prayers. Beitris started to react to her demand and moaned as she expelled the bairn from her body. Sorcha pulled it free, and her concern grew. The bairn wasn't crying and dinna open his eyes.

"Is something wrong?" Beitris asked. "Do I have a son or a daughter?"

She wanted to deliver the good news she had a braw son, but she was afraid she had to give her some bad tidings. "He's not breathing."

"Make him," Beitris demanded, her tone full of panic. She gestured toward the baby. "Give him tae me."

Sorcha cleaned him and wrapped him up in a small blanket then handed him over to Beitris. She should be able to see her wee one even if he hadn't stood a chance. The vicar should've reacted quicker than he had. Maybe then she'd have been able to save the babe.

"Ye did this," Beitris said. "He'd have lived if not

for yer insistence I push him out when I did. He needed more time."

Beitris's agony and grief rushed over her, making Sorcha stumble back as the emotions hit her hard. She reached out for something to steady her balance, but couldn't find anything. If she didn't find her breath soon, she might lose consciousness. "Ye dinna believe that."

"Woman, ye be all right?" Tamhas Gall asked his wife as he stepped into the room. "Is it done?" He had a stony expression on his face. Gone was the gentleman filled with anxiety who'd come to fetch her earlier. This man before her didn't remotely resemble him. How could one person be such a mix of contrary emotions? The vicar was so heartless it almost crushed her. Did he not care for his wife and child? He walked over to Beitris's side and picked up the swaddled bairn from her arms. "Why isn't it crying?"

"She killed him," Beitris accused, completely hysterical as she screeched the words. "He never had a chance."

Tamhas set the bairn into Beitris's arms. "I should never have gone tae ye for help. Ye be a witch as the rumors say. Ye'll pay for yer sins." His voice was accusatory mixed with contempt. His eyes narrowed into tiny slits. Malice poured out of him in waves as he stalked forward.

He picked up a pot and swung it at Sorcha, the

blow landed across her face. The bones in her nose cracked on impact, and her face became wet from her own blood. The room spun around her, and she lost all control she had. The emotions in the room overloaded her and—along with the physical blow—undid her. Blackness took over, leaving her easy prey to the one man she feared would be the death of her.

CHAPTER 2

Visions came to Caitrìona when she least expected them. Sometimes she understood their meaning, and others were so obscure she could only guess. Most of the time they were things yet to pass, but every now and then, it was a bit of the past, as if some higher being was attempting to prevent her from making the same mistake made by another. Either way, Caitrìona Dalais Guaire, always took what was shown to her seriously.

So, when she was sitting in her cottage with the wee twins, doing a little embroidery in the late afternoon sunlight, she paused to take note of the one that rolled through her. The vision was more a series of flashes that didn't mean much to her and the first one was of her dear sister, Sorcha, with a babe in her arms. The room unfamiliar, but the other occupants were the vicar and his wife; however, the import of it was lost on her.

The next one was of her husband's blacksmith shop. Caitrìona stood in the middle of it with the sun setting in the horizon, wearing the same dress she currently wore—suggesting something would happen later that day. She glanced up as someone approached, their fist poised to strike. The pain of the blow connected with her even through the vision. It hurt, but she believed the pain was dulled because of the vision state. When it happened in truth, she'd probably lose consciousness. If she could prevent it, she would.

The next vision was of her husband. He stood on the outskirts of the field leading to Dalais Manor. An angry mob of villagers descended upon it. Torches lit up the night sky as they pounded on the door. Her brother, Niall, opened them wide and addressed the rabble gathered outside. Not long after, they carried him off. Her brother didn't fight them and appeared to accept his fate.

Fear spread through her belly like wildfire, consuming everything in its path. If this was to come... She swallowed hard as the next image rolled through her. It was of Ailis. She was crouched below in a hidden cellar in Dalais manor. She held Lachlan and the twins in her arms. A silent tear fell down her cheek. Ailis lifted her hand and wiped it away. She leaned down and kissed each child's cheek, whispering some words to them. She held up a finger to her mouth, perhaps to coax them to be quiet. They were definitely hiding from someone.

The why of it all was lost on her. Caitrìona didn't understand the reasons the mob had for carrying her brother off. Ailis had looked so terrified as she stared up at the closed latch of the cellar. Were the mob after her and the wee ones? Who would protect them? In that moment, she understood exactly what she must do. All the images, save the one of Sorcha, were later in the day. Sorcha's must be a past vision, and the rest the future.

She could do something to help her brother and his wife. She might even be able to save herself. Only God could help her dear sister now. She dreaded what fate might befall Sorcha, and she hated to think of it. People feared what they didn't understand, and Sorcha would pay a heavy price for their super-stitions.

Caitrìona stood abruptly and called out to the girls, "Come my wee lasses, we're tae visit Dalais today." The girls happily hopped over to her and they started their journey toward the manor. The walk would take them less than a half-hour, but it seemed as if it would take all day.

Her twin daughters were identical down to the dimples in their left cheek and the white-blonde hair that fell past their ears in soft curls. Wee lasses of no more than four, they had much growing to do. Her braw husband believed they looked like her and would steal the hearts of all the young men around them. They did have her coloring, but she didn't see much else of her in them.

"Ma," little Moire said.

"Yes, dear one," she replied.

"Will Uncle Niall play with us?"

Her daughters loved their uncle. He doted on them whenever they visited. Niall was Caitrìona's twin, and they had a special bond. That connection had carried over to her daughters.

"Love Uncle Niall," Lili said happily.

"He'll be glad ye both want tae see him," she said. "But I dinna ken what his plans are for the day. That's what I need be finding out."

She prayed she had enough time to go to Dalais, and then to the blacksmith shop. Caitrìona feared if she missed Daniel, he'd pay the price she'd received in the vision she'd had. She wouldn't be able to forgive herself if he was hurt in her stead. It had to be prevented—all of it.

Dalais manor filled the horizon. Her family home had always held a special place in her heart. How could it not? She'd spent her early days growing in its hallowed halls. Her mother had died giving birth to Niall and her—they were twins, but not identical like her daughters. Sorcha was the eldest child and had always taken care of them in little ways. They'd had a nurse who was in charge of their care, but Sorcha was their heart. Their father had taken little interest in them. They were so close to reaching their destination. A few more steps and she'd be inside, and hopefully she'd find Niall there.

She climbed the steps with the twins at her side. It didn't take them long to reach the top. They arrived at the door a few moments later. Caitrìona pushed it open and gestured for the twins to go inside. "Ailis," she called out. A few moments later, Ailis came out with Lachlan at her side. Caitrìona scrunched her eyebrows together in confusion. "Sorcha's been here already then?" She thought she might have, but had hoped maybe she'd been wrong.

"Aye," Ailis said. "She brought the wee lad several hours ago. The vicar's wife is birthing her bairn."

The vision of Sorcha had actually come to pass. Caitrìona didn't quite understand it. What did the birth of a bairn have to do with the other visions? The only connection between the blacksmith shop and the mob at Dalais Manor was her family. "Would ye mind keeping the wee lasses too? I've something of import I must do." She hoped she wasn't fulfilling the prophecy instead of attempting to thwart it. Though, either way, it didn't really matter as long as her girls stayed safe—they were more important than her own life.

"I dinna mind," she said. "It's good practice for

when my own bairn comes." She rubbed her hand over her belly.

"How is my wee nephew?" Caitrìona placed her hand over Ailis's belly. The bairn kicked her in greeting and she laughed. "He's going tae be a braw one." Caitrìona had once had a vision of Ailis's bairn after he'd been born. She'd been standing over a cradle, smiling down at him. She had looked up at someone and said the bairn's name. When Caitrìona had mentioned the name from her vision, both Ailis and Niall had loved it. They hadn't dared speak it aloud again for fear it would not come to pass. When the wee one entered the world, they'd say it again to celebrate his birth. "I'll return as soon as I am able."

Ailis nodded. "We'll be waiting. Go, the wee lasses will be fine here with me and Lachlan."

Caitrìona nodded and turned to leave. She kept her pace even as she headed out the door. Everything inside of her screamed to run as fast as possible to the blacksmith shop—to Daniel. She didn't want to frighten the twins or Ailis though. The twins were too young to understand Caitrìona's visions, but Ailis would ken immediately something wasn't right. So, she waited until she gained a bit of distance from the manor before she gave into the urge. Then she ran as fast as her legs would take her. She wished she had a carriage for traveling. It would help if she could get their faster, but that was impossible, as she didn't have access to one. She would have to use what she had and pray it would be enough. The town was a couple miles from Dalais and a quick hike if she didn't dally.

She didn't stop once until she reached the outskirt of the village, and only then did she slow her pace. As she walked through the street, she glanced back and forth between the villagers. No one bothered to look at her, and she breathed a sigh of relief. She wasn't too late. Then something caught her attention.

A group of people were milling around the entrance of the church yard. The vicar shouted at them, and they yelled back. The fear she'd felt earlier returned in full force. What was the vicar doing? Why wasn't he at his home with his wife?

Caitrìona rushed forward and ducked inside the blacksmith shop. Whatever was happening, she wasn't going to be able to stop it. There was nothing she could do except make sure everything was on the correct path. A stabbing pain shot through Caitrìona's head as a flash of her sister forced itself into her mind. Blood dripped from a crack in her lip and a dark bruise formed on her left cheek in angry colors of red, blue, and green. Tears pooled in her eyes as sobs resonated around her. Her surroundings left little to be desired. The room was dark, damp, and encased in dirt. A small narrow window offered her little light. Caitrìona shook the images away and raised her hand to her chest attempting to still her rapidly beating heart. Her dear sister... Sorcha was already lost, and Caitrìona already grieved for her. Saving herself was out of the question now too. She could only save her children and her husband. She would have to be all right with that. A lump formed in her throat and she swallowed it down. There was no time for feeling sorry for herself.

"Daniel," she called out.

"Back here," he replied.

She stepped through to the backroom where he was working on a small dirk. Daniel held it in place with a pair of tongs and beat it with a hammer. He dipped it into a barrel of water and then placed it on a stone surface, studying the workmanship.

"Daniel," she stepped closer. "Can ye please look at me?"

Her husband was a braw man. She'd always thought him handsome and strong. The long hours he pounded metals into various items had shaped his muscles into works of art themselves. She appreciated his body and his gorgeous face, but that hadn't been why she'd fallen in love with him. His giving nature and innate kindness had drawn her to his side. When he had wooed her with his charm and enticing smile, she'd been lost. There would be no other man for her. It didn't matter that he'd been beneath her and she'd never be a grand lady. None of that had ever mattered to her. She had loved him and always would.

"What ye need, lass? He asked absentmindedly as he worked. His tone was soft though, and his love for her echoed through it. He'd never completely ignore her. They had a strong bond.

"I've had a vision," she told him.

That was all he needed to set the dirk aside and come to her. "What did ye see?" Everyone in the family took her visions seriously. They had enough experience to realize that what she saw would eventually come to pass. "Ye have no color in ye lovely face. Is it so bad?"

She nodded and sucked in a breath to hold back the tears. This would be the last time she saw her beautiful husband. Caitrìona wanted to have this one moment to carry with her to remember him by. His sweetness, concern, and love... She leaned forward and pressed her lips to his. Their warmth seeped into her and eased some of the coldness that had settled into her stomach. "I dinna have time to explain everything," she said as she stepped back. Ye must do as I tell ye."

"All right," he agreed warily.

"Go tae Dalais," she said. "Now, while there is still time. Ye must save Ailis and the bairns."

He crinkled his brow. "The wee lasses?"

"Aye," she replied. "And Lachlan."

"Where is ye brother?"

She shook her head. There was no time for this. She hadn't asked Ailis where Niall was when she'd been at the manor. It hadn't occurred to her. When she'd realized the connections, she'd had to act fast. In her haste, she hadn't taken in the whole picture. She realized now she should have told Ailis about her vision too.

"Ye'll see when ye arrive," she said.

If she told him too much it might prevent him from doing what he must. He couldn't know that when he arrived he'd see the mob walk off with Niall in their arms. He might try to quicken his pace and try to save him. The mob would end up with two victims for their plans. Daniel had to save Ailis and the bairns. They were far more important.

"Where ye be goin?" he asked.

"I have tae find Sorcha," she lied. She had a feeling she'd be seeing her soon, but not in a hospitable environment. She dreaded that moment more than she could ever express. It would be filled with terror and pain beyond what she wanted to think about. Her fate had been sealed long before she had that vision. It broke her heart and shredded her to her very soul. This was her last moment with the man she loved. She'd likely never see him again or her dear girls. She had to protect him, and their daughters. She might not be able to stop what fate had in store for her, but she could do her very best to ensure their survival. "Promise me ye'll save them."

"Aye," he said. Then leaned down to kiss her

quickly. "They'll be fine, my love. Don't worry ye bonny head about it."

"The cellar in the back of the kitchen," she said. "Go there when it's safe."

With those words, he left through the back door of the shop. It clicked shut, and a few moments later, she heard the door open at the front. She turned toward the sound and met the gaze of Ellair Friseal, one of the vicar's close friends. He was mean spirited and abused everyone and everything around him.

"Ellair," she said, surprised. "If ye be looking for Daniel, he's closed shop for the day. There's been a family emergency." It was late afternoon and her husband almost never closed this early. She hoped Ellair would leave without incident, but she doubted he'd come for the blacksmith's services.

"I'll speak with ye husband later," he said. "It's ye that I'm here for. We noticed ye heading in this direction. Saves us time in looking for ye later."

Then he raised his fist and punched her in the face. He was the one from her vision... It didn't surprise her, but she'd hope to avoid the pain of being hit. Sadly, she'd been right, and it did hurt more than it had in the vision. The world went black as she fell backward.

CHAPTER 3

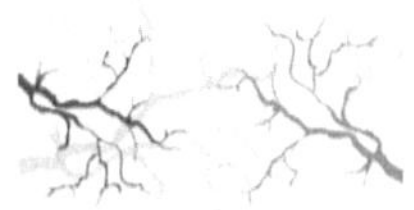

Niall, Baron of Dalais sat on top of his horse and surveyed the land. The tenants' farms were doing all right, and he expected the harvest to go well at the end of the month. He'd been out all day talking to the farmers and making sure they had everything they needed. He'd started to become acquainted with the tenants as a wee lad and had taken over most of the duties when he was a young man. His father had slowly lost interest in running the barony and had given him complete control well before his death a few years ago.

Sometimes, the responsibilities of his station grated on him. There were days he wished he could take his family and head to a different place. The changes in Scotland bothered him on a visceral level. It ached deep inside as he interpreted the rot surrounding people. They took the newfound attitude toward witches as a reason to persecute innocents in the name of God. Their own evil hearts belied their true beliefs, and they didn't realize it. He saw it in the color surrounding their souls.

In the distance, shouts echoed, catching his attention. He turned toward the sound and noticed a large group of people heading toward Dalais Manor. Their intentions screamed loudly at him, not by their voices, but the bright red hue around them. Anger and viciousness overflowed, tinting each member of the mob. Niall kicked his horse into a gallop, heading toward the manor. He had to arrive before the mob. He didn't understand why they were on their way to his home, but he had to be there to protect Ailis and their unborn son.

He stopped at the front of the manor, hopped off the horse, and took the time to quickly tether it to a nearby hitching post. Niall rushed inside and headed to the sitting room where Ailis preferred to do her needlework. When he walked inside he stopped short when she was nowhere to be found. His heart raced hard inside his chest. He spun on his heels and exited the room, moving toward the staircase.

"Ailis," he shouted.

"In the nursery," she yelled back.

He took the stairs two at a time as he ran up to the nursery. She must be preparing something for the bairn when it arrived. Why else would she be in that particular room? When he went inside, he was surprised to find his twin nieces and Lachlan with her. His wife was in the middle of telling them a tale of adventure and bravery.

"Ailis," he said urgently. "I must speak with ye now."

"Can it wait?"

"Nay," he said. "Bring the wee ones and follow me"

Ailis didn't move. She pursed her lips together in displeasure. "They've had a long day and must rest for the night."

He didn't have time for this. He had to make them move. The mob would be there soon, and when they arrived... Niall shook his head. He didn't want to think about what might happen if they made it through the doors of Dalais. Ailis and the bairns had to be safe. They were all that mattered.

"I ken they're tired, love," he said softly. "But I wouldn't be dragging ye or them away if it wasn't necessary."

Niall didn't wait for her to reply. He walked over to one of the beds and scooped Moire and Lili into his arms. Ailis reluctantly lifted Lachlan up and followed him out the door. He led them down to the servants' stairs and to the kitchen, then pushed open the door to the cool pantry. In the far back, there was a brass ring that opened a cellar door. They didn't use this part of the house much. Niall couldn't afford to hire servants full time. A maid came three times a week to help Ailis with the cleaning, but the house was taken care of, in large, by his wife.

He set the wee lasses down and lifted the brass ring. "Ye must climb inside," he insisted.

"Why?" Ailis asked. Her hands shook, and she started to fidget. She glanced around the room as if trying to figure out what could possibly be so urgent. His wife wasn't a fool and had to realize there'd be a good reason his sisters had left their children in her care. It wasn't the first time they'd done so, but not without giving her some notice. Niall hadn't expected to find them there, and they certainly didn't spend the night often. Caitrìona and Sorcha both hated being separated from their children. They wouldn't have left them at Dalais if they weren't in trouble, and that same danger had found its way to his doorstep. "What is it?"

"There be an angry mob heading toward the house. I don't ken yet what they be wanting, but I won't put ye or the wee ones at risk."

She clutched on to his shirt, terror filling her features. "Sorcha came by to ask me to watch Lachlan. She was going to help the vicar's wife deliver her bairn."

Niall understood her meaning immediately. If Sorcha used any of her special gifts, it would have immediately outed her as a witch in the eyes of those who believed in such things. "How long ago was that?

"Early afternoon," she said. "Not long after Caitrìona came by. She asked me tae look after the twins. She had a vision."

He cursed under his breath. That was not a good sign at all. She must have had an idea of what was to come. "Did she tell ye anything?"

Ailis shook her head. "She dinna say she had a vision. I could tell by the look of her. She was in a might hurry to be somewhere, and I ken she would explain when she could. Ye ken how her visions are."

Pounding on the door reverberated through the manor. The irate group of people had arrived. The time to discuss things had ended. Niall kissed his wife quickly and pulled away from her. He would deal with the mob and then figure out what happened with his sisters. He couldn't handle more than one thing at a time, and at that moment, it was more important to see to Ailis and the wee ones. "Quick, crawl down inside. When it's safe, I'll open the latch and let ye out."

Ailis didn't argue this time. She slid down into the cellar and reached up to help the wee ones down. First, he handed her Moire, then her twin sister, Lili. When the girls were settled, he handed her Lachlan. Then he closed the lid to the cellar and placed a nearby rug over it. If, for some reason, the house was searched, they wouldn't think to look for them down there. Ailis could escape it after a time if necessary, but she'd wait until she had no choice.

Niall hated leaving her down there; however, if it saved her life along with the bairns, he'd be glad for it.

He left the cellar and headed toward the front of the house. When he reached the parlor, the door swung open and Tamhas Gall walked through the entrance. Several men came in behind him. They glowed red, and their fury almost knocked Niall over. So much hatred permeated these men's souls. How could they live with themselves?

"Do ye walk in uninvited often?" Niall raised a brow. "What can I do for ye?"

"Where is ye lady wife?" Tamhas asked.

"She's not here at present," Niall lied. He hated lying, but he'd do anything for his love. "She's gone tae visit family in Edinburgh. What do ye need her for?"

"We need tae speak with her," Tamhas said. "Fetch her now. We mean her no harm. She was here earlier when I visited. It is of great import."

His lies tinged the red around him a bright yellow. If he found Ailis, he would definitely hurt her. Niall would die before he told him where to find his beloved. They would not find her, and she would be long gone before they had a chance to ken she'd been at Dalais Manor all along.

"As I told ye," he said calmly. "She's visiting family and left some time ago. It must have been after you called." He hoped the vicar believed him.

Ailis and the bairns's lives depended upon it. "Ye may leave the way ye came."

Tamhas glanced around him and then smiled evilly at Niall. "We'll catch up with her later. She can't have gone far." Tamhas replied with contempt. His lips turned up into an evil smile as he met Niall's gaze. "Ye'll be coming with us."

Niall lifted a brow mockingly. "By who's authority? I'm the highest-ranking peer in this county. I dinna have tae answer tae ye."

It wouldn't matter in the end. He might be the baron, but this crowd wouldn't care. He could see it in their eyes, and even without his special gifts. They were bloodthirsty, and they'd see him dead. They probably already had both of his sisters. Why the family was targeted as a whole, he couldn't be sure. If Sorcha had used her healing gifts on the vicar's wife...

The vicar didn't like him or his sisters and took every opportunity to tell anyone who'd listen. Something must have happened to give him the leverage he'd been craving to act against them. Niall couldn't be sure what the vicar had discovered. Either way, it wasn't good, and his family would pay the price. He couldn't help thinking Tamhas had somehow planned it. The vicar was malicious to the depths of his soul, and Niall had known it since the first time he'd met him. He'd warned his sisters about Tamhas's treachery and told them to avoid the man.

Sorcha and her kind heart believed the man could be saved. But there was no helping a man like the vicar; he was beyond redemption.

"I answer to a higher authority than ye," the vicar said, then sneered. "By the king's decree, anyone suspected of witchcraft is to be brought to trial, and if so judged a witch, sentenced to death."

Niall almost snorted at his speech. For a moment, he thought the man would bring God down as his higher authority. He was supposed to speak for the higher being, after all. Alas, nay, this man was using the king's superstitions for his own evil plans. It didn't surprise Niall at all. "Ye suspect me of this witch nonsense? What evidence are ye charging me with?"

He'd done nothing to give this man, or anyone, any indication he had a special gift. Their family was careful and didn't let any outsiders know of what their family bloodline carried inside of it. The wee ones were already starting to show signs that they had gifts of their own. It was why Caitrìona and Sorcha had decided they would not attend the village school until they could be tutored to hide what made them special.

"Yer sisters are already in custody and soon they will confess their sins," Tamhas declared. "We only need one thing to prove yer a witch. If ye carry the mark of the devil, it will damn ye."

What the bloody hell was he going on about

now? There was no such thing as a mark... Then he remembered. They all had a birthmark. They were each unique and similar at the same time. It was a strawberry mark, the shape of a complete circle. There was a pointed tip on one side of each one. His was at the very top of the circle, Sorcha's on the left bottom corner, and Caitrìona's the right bottom corner. If they were to be placed on top of each other the marks would almost look like a triangle inter-twined with a circle. They were three parts making up the whole...

"We already saw it on Sorcha's left shoulder," Tamhas boasted. "Ellair Friseal is bringing in Caitrìona. He'll find her mark before he brings her in. Do ye want to make it easy on yerself and show us yer mark now?"

Caitrìona's mark was on her ankle. Niall's was on his thigh. He wasn't about to strip in front of these men and show it to them. "I must decline yer ridicu-lous offer."

"Have it yer way," Tamhas said. "Ye will be showing it to us soon enough."

"It's a *sair fecht,*" Niall whispered under his breath, accepting his fate.

The men descended on Dalais Manor and tore at Niall's clothing. He was helpless to stop them. They carried him near naked across the fields of his home and didn't stop until they reached the village church. There, they deposited him into a room with a dirt floor. He glanced up and into the eyes of his two sisters.

Caitrìona and Sorcha were wearing torn clothing as well and each had a bruised face. They cried when they saw him, and he pulled them into his arms. Sorrow clamored through his whole body as he realized how doomed the three of them were. Niall didn't understand why they had been thrust into such a terrible fate; however, he was certain of one thing. His sisters needed him and he would have to find strength somehow to see them through the impending disaster. For this was only the beginning, and he feared the worst was yet to come.

CHAPTER 4

Night had fallen shortly after he left the blacksmith shop and headed toward Dalais Manor. Daniel Guaire strolled at an even pace, unsure if he should hurry or not. Caitrìona's visions were nothing to be trifled with. She'd saved his life once because of her gift. If anyone found out about what made her special though—he'd not think of it. If she told him to do something because of her visions, he did without question—even if everything inside of him screamed something wasn't right.

His wife was beautiful and kind—Daniel fell in love with her the moment he met her and not just because of her appearance. Though that didn't hurt... Caitrìona had dark blue eyes, white blonde hair, and lush curves. He'd never tire of gazing upon her fair visage. His wife was beautiful inside and out. It had been her fair beauty that had first caught his attention, but her innate goodness had captured his heart.

All of the Dalais siblings had a special gift. It was their family secret, and once he'd become a part of their family, it'd become his to keep as well. He understood why it had to be that way. The king had come back from his travels extra superstitious, believing witchcraft responsible for the storms on his voyage. That erroneous conclusion spread wide through Scotland and beyond. But in Scotland, it was illegal to practice the dark arts.

None of the Dalais siblings were actual witches. They didn't worship any dark being, and they had no actual magical abilities. If they were a coven, then by proxy, so was he, along with Ailis and Brian. If they stretched their superstitions far enough, the witch hunters might even include the wee ones. They were the true innocents in it all. They'd not asked to be born. They were already showing signs of having a gift of their own. Little Moire, his dear wee one, had the sight, and Lili was too sensitive for her own good.

Caitrìona believed Lili was developing an empathy gift similar to Sorcha's. She was too attuned to the feelings of everyone around her. She often started crying without reason and hugged her mother. Lachlan, the poor wee lad, had energy to burn. They couldn't be certain, but he might carry more than one of the abilities. After much discussion, they'd agreed to keep a close eye on him. One gift was hard enough, but all of them?

Daniel walked over a hill and stopped suddenly. In the distance, he could see torchlight glittering in the night sky. Shouts echoed though the wind, chilling his bones. Was this why Caitrìona had sent him? She'd said he'd ken it when he arrived. His children, his sweet wee lasses, were inside Dalais Manor. That mob didn't appear to be the friendly sort. If they harmed them...

He didn't ken what kind of man would harm a small child, but he believed to his very soul those men would kill anyone in their path. If he stormed to the manor, they'd trample over him, and then what good would he be? Caitrìona had asked him to save the wee ones and Ailis. She hadn't mentioned her brother.

A ruckus riled the crowd, and they stormed the manor. Daniel couldn't drag his gaze away from the horror. They shouted with maddening glee as they destroyed anything they could lift or smash. He feared they might take the torches to the manor and burn it to the ground. Daniel prayed they would not take it that far. He had to hope that Caitrìona would have warned him of that possibility. Another set of movements caught his attention. He turned his head back to the entrance to the manor. The vicar was at the head of it, shouting at the other men. They had another male in their possession. At first, they carried him outside, then they began to drag him along the ground. His clothes were torn and his face was almost unrecognizable, but to Daniel it was clear who they hauled along the ground.

Daniel sucked in a sickened breath. His stomach rolled inside of him, and he finally understood why Caitrìona wasn't with him. Their secret was out somehow, and they were being brought in as witches. His dear sweet wife had thought to protect him instead of saving herself. She didn't run away. God, he wished she had... Instead, she'd run to him and did everything she could to save the children. Ailis... She was pregnant with her first child. That bairn was to be the heir to Dalais. Sadly, there might not be much for him to inherit after the witch trials concluded. If they kept to their pattern, they would arrest everyone in the family that was close to the accused. No one was safe, and he suspected Caitrìona feared they'd harm him, or the bairns. They certainly wouldn't have held back where Ailis was concerned, pregnant or not.

The men cheered as they neared him. He waited in silence as the group started to pass. He kept hidden behind a nearby tree and tried to calm his rapid heartbeat. His stomach pained him as it filled with dread. Why hadn't his dear wife told him what would happen? Probably because she'd known he would not have left her behind. He didn't believe for a moment that she was safe. They were attacking

Dalais—the highest-ranking lord in the county. That meant no one was safe and the whole family faced unimaginable danger. He didn't have time to mourn his fate or go back for his wife. She'd given him one task—save the children. He wouldn't fail her or them. Later, he'd allow himself the time to grieve what he'd lost. Until then, he had to stay focused.

He stared at the men as they walked by him. Their angry shouts echoed around him. The rotten bastards should be the ones punished for their decrepit souls. Caitrìona, Sorcha, and Niall were good, honest people. How could they not see that? They would claim the three siblings had bespelled him with their magic to believe they were not witches, but they hadn't. Daniel dinna ken how these men could be so evil. He wasn't sure he wanted to.

After several excruciating minutes, the last of the mob passed by. Daniel crept forward, trying his best to remain silent in his movements. He made his way to the manor door. It was still wide open, and the foyer had been ripped to shreds. Someone had even slashed through a painting, and a few vases had been smashed on the floor. It was a wonder they hadn't thought to set fire to the manor itself. Daniel was grateful they hadn't.

He walked through the main rooms and checked everywhere he thought Ailis and the wee ones might be. The men must've had a similar thought. Not one room in the manor had gone untouched by their invasion. It wasn't until he reached the bottom of the stairs that he remembered the last thing Caitrìona had said to him.

Daniel ran to the kitchen and into the pantry, then scanned the floor. A rug he wasn't used to seeing at the end caught his attention. It had been kicked a little as the mob searched the house, but it had hidden what it was intended to. They hadn't kicked it enough... He yanked the rug away from the cellar door and lifted the latch. Inside he found Ailis, the twins, and Lachlan. Ailis's face was tear stained, her midnight tresses falling down her back in tangles, she rubbed her belly with one hand, and the other rested over her chest.

"Och, Daniel," she said surprised. "Ye nearly had my heart beating out of my chest."

"Ye have had a scare this day," he said. "It's not over yet. Hand me a wee one so we can make haste." Daniel reached down and Ailis gave him one of the twins. He set her down and lifted the other out. After all the wee ones were safe, Daniel reached to help Ailis out too. The kids were quiet and stared at him for a long while. He didn't question their behavior. They had gifts like their mothers' and had probably discerned in some way the gravity of their situation. It made him sick that they understood, even remotely, that danger lurked around them. Children should only know happy things and play safe in their own homes.

But these wee ones had a lifetime of hurt to endure.

"Where's Niall?" Ailis asked.

He didn't want to tell her what happened to her husband. As they had passed, he was able to get a better look at him, and it hadn't been pretty. His face had been black and blue, and not all of that was from the dirt he collected as they dragged his limp body. Daniel wasn't even sure the man had still been breathing. In some ways, it would've been a relief for him to already be dead. What they had in store for him would be far worse in the end.

Deep down he realized Caitrìona had a similar fate, and he'd have to explain it to his daughters some day. He didn't want to think about his future or what was probably already happening to his wife. His mind would retreat to a dark place, and he wouldn't be able to help what remained of his family. As much as it hurt him to shove those feelings aside—Daniel understood his role and played it through.

Daniel shook his head. "It's not good."

Tears fell over her cheeks once again. She hiccupped as she fought to catch her breath. "Is he..."

"I ken not," he said. "But we canna stay here tae find out. They'll be looking for ye and the bairns. We must get ye to a safe place."

Ailis looked down at the children then back up at him. He could tell the moment when she gathered enough strength to continue on. She stood straighter, and her mouth formed a thin line. She held her hand on her belly and met his gaze. "I'll pack a few provisions. We're going to need them if we're traveling."

"Not a lot," he warned. "We're going to have to go on foot until we reach the next village. Once there, we'll make a plan on where to go next."

Sailing to France might be their best option. They might not ever be able to return home, but the wee ones would be safe. The witch hunters of Scotland wouldn't think to look for them there. It was more likely they'd look in a neighboring village or as far as England. But France—that was a little farther to travel to hunt someone they believed of worshipping a dark entity.

"Aye," Ailis agreed. "We'll need some food for the journey. I'll grab a few small valuables too. We'll need to sell them for money."

Ailis left him alone with the bairns. He took them to the kitchen and set them down at the table. Lachlan rubbed his eyes with his fists. "I'm tired," he yawned. "Can I sleep yet?"

"In a little while," he told the lad.

"Da," Moire said.

"Yes, poppet," he replied.

She was so much like his wife, his heart hurt looking at her. The same brilliant blue eyes and white blonde hair—Daniel wanted to wrap his arms around both of his daughters and cry for what they were losing. If he could change things, he would, but now wasn't the time for maudlin thinking. He had to take control and lead what was left of his family to safety. Once they were secure, he could come back and maybe save his wife. He doubted he could, but he had to try.

"I'm hungry," Moire told him.

"Would ye like a slice of bread and jam?"

She nodded happily. He sliced some bread that sat on a nearby counter next to a jar of tomato jam. After spreading jam on the slices, he gave each of the wee ones a piece. The other two hadn't asked for anything to eat, but it was inevitable once Moire started to eat hers. They each picked up their bread and chewed quietly.

Ailis came back shortly with a small bag. He didn't ask her what was in it. When she was ready to tell him, she would. She went to the pantry then grabbed a basket and filled it with fruit, cheese, and a fresh loaf of bread. Enough food for them until they reached the village, and maybe a little extra for the next part of their journey.

"I'm ready," she said.

Daniel nodded and turned to the bairns. "Are ye done eating?"

They all bobbed their heads at once. "Is it time to sleep now?" Lachlan asked.

He wished he could tell the lad it was. "We're going on an adventure," Daniel explained. "Dinna ye like to play that game with yer ma?"

Lachlan smiled. "Is ma coming too?"

His heart broke. The poor lad might never see either one of his parents again. Daniel had no idea where Brian was. Caitrìona had instructed him to save Ailis and the wee ones. She left the rest of the adults to whatever fate had in store for them.

"Not this time," he said sadly. "Come on now, we must begin."

The children followed behind him in silence. He suspected the twins understood far more than they were saying. Lachlan might even as well, but hadn't been willing to believe it. In time, he'd trust his instincts. The wee ones would have to grow up much sooner than they should have. Daniel would've changed that for them if he could.

Ailis put her small bag inside the basket. She took Lachlan's hand in hers, and carried the basket of food in the other, then nodded at Daniel. "After ye," she said.

Daniel reached down and picked up Moire's hand, then Lili's. They were a solemn group as the left Dalais Manor for perhaps the last time. He didn't look back, not once. It was too painful, and his heart had already been shredded enough for one lifetime.

CHAPTER 5

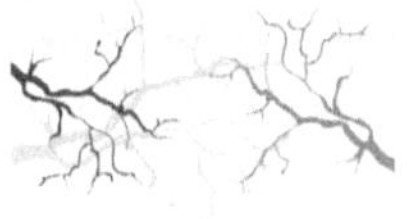

Two weeks later…

Caitrìona, Sorcha, and Niall were dragged out of their cell and pushed out into the court-yard. The sun blinded Caitrìona, and she stumbled forward, hitting the ground hard. Pain had become a constant companion of hers in the hell she'd been subjected to, alongside her brother and sister. If she could've enacted a curse on the evil individuals who'd tortured them, she would.

"Get up, ye evil wicked witch," Tamhas ordered. "Ye'll not fool us in tae believing ye ever again. Ye will not pray tae yer evil master."

Tamhas Gall was the only evil thing she was acquainted with, and she'd rather stab her own eyes out than worship him. Catriona slowly stood and met his gaze with as much defiance as she could muster, then spat in his face. She smiled for the first time in days at the horror that filled his features. He wiped the spit away and then glared at her.

"Ye'll pay for that."

"What can ye do tae me that ye haven't already?" She laughed maniacally. "Are we not already sentenced tae die this day?"

"Cat, *haud yer wheesht*," Sorcha said sharply.

"No, let her," Niall said. "They might be about tae murder us, but we dinna have tae make it easy for them."

Sorcha closed her eyes and a tear slipped down her cheek. Her usually lovely fiery red hair was dull and stained with dirt. They'd been tortured for days. If they confessed, they'd be spared a trial and their sentence carried out immediately. Their pain and suffering would end. Why not make their lives easier? Not one of the three siblings had bothered to reply to that tirade. They endured for reasons the likes of Tamhas Gall would never understand.

The longer Tamhas kept his attention on them, the more time Daniel and Ailis had to escape with the wee ones. None of them wanted what happened to Brian to befall the rest of their family. Poor Brian had been hit so hard he'd been dead before he hit the floor of the shop. The vicar had been a little too gleeful when describing how Sorcha's husband died. By then, Sorcha was numb and had found a way to close her gift from being used. Otherwise, she'd have been tortured far greater than anything Tamhas could've done to her physically or otherwise.

"Yer ready tae return tae hell?" Tamhas asked. "I'll be glad tae send ye there."

Niall didn't turn his gaze to him. The muscles in his cheek twitched, but he didn't move an inch. He probably didn't want to give Tamhas the satisfaction of realizing he'd hit a sore spot. Caitrìona couldn't blame her brother. Spitting at Tamhas had felt good. The only thing better would be finding out this had all been a horrible nightmare.

"If I'm sentenced tae hell, then I'll gladly wait until ye join me so I may witness the torture ye'll find at the hands of the dark one," Niall said.

"Have ye cursed me?" The color drained from Tamhas's face.

"Nay," Niall said. "Ye have yerself tae blame for yer fate."

"Tie them tae the pyre," Tamhas ordered. "It's time tae send them tae their graves for their sins."

All of them were pushed toward the large wooden stakes that had been erected in the court-yard. Kindling had been piled around them. A large burly man pulled her forward and tied her to the post—her siblings flanked either side of her bound to their own stake. Rope tore into her flesh he'd tied it so tight. She whimpered in pain. The sun appeared to brighten in the sky as Caitrìona's vision darkened. Her head rolled back as a vision struck her. How appropriate. On the cusp of her death, she'd receive one final peek into the future.

"Isn't he beautiful?" Ailis asked. "My little Samuel." She leaned down and kissed his forehead. "If only yer da could be here tae see ye." She glanced up and met someone's gaze. "Do ye wish tae hold him?"

"Aye," Daniel said as he stepped over tae the bed. "He's a fine bairn. Niall would've been a proud da."

A tear fell down Ailis's cheek. She wiped it away and smiled softly. "I miss him terribly."

Daniel fidgeted with the bairn's blanket and didn't meet Ailis's gaze. He appeared to be fighting his own tears. The wee one started to fuss in his arms and he whispered softly to him, "Dinna fash yerself, wee Samuel," he said. "I'll always be here for ye."

The bairn stopped crying and stared up at Daniel. He was an intelligent lad for being newly born. It was almost as if he understood what Daniel had been saying. That couldn't be right though. Wee ones didn't start to ken the world around them for years. Daniel handed the bairn back to Ailis.

"He wants his ma," he said.

"Ye have a way with wee ones," Ailis replied. "I'm glad yer here with me. I dinna think I'd survive without ye."

"Ye'd have been fine," Daniel said gruffly. "And ye'll make a wonderful ma tae the wee one."

Ailis stared down at Samuel and smiled. "If I

didn't have him, I'd not have had a reason tae go on. Without Niall..."

Daniel had his back to Ailis. He didn't move for several moments, then he turned toward her. He swallowed hard before he spoke again. His eyes held a hint of sadness that hadn't been there before. He wasn't broken, but he wasn't whole either. "I miss my Cat," he whispered. "I always will. I dinna arrive in time tae save her. I'll always regret that."

"There's nothing ye could've done," Ailis told him. "Ye'd have died as well."

He shook his head. "Sometimes I think that would've been preferable. But, Aye," he agreed. "There was no saving them from that pyre. It's a horror that I won't soon forget."

This time a tear did escape from the corner of his eye. He gave into the sobs, letting them wrack through his whole body. A strong man in tears was something to behold. He sat down in a chair and leaned down as he finally gave into the agony of losing the woman he loved. When the well of tears started to dry, he leaned back and wiped his face. He met Ailis's gaze. "I think we should marry and change our names. For the sake of the children. They need a life that's not tainted by the death of their parents."

"They didn't lose all of them," Ailis quietly reminded him. "We're still here."

"Aye," he said. "And we always will be."

She nodded. "What would we call ourselves?"

"Noble," he said. "It has a nice sound tae it."

She smiled. "Aye, it does."

Caitrìona blinked several times as the vision washed away. Her face was wet with her own tears. Somewhere out there in the crowd was her dear Daniel—or he would be. She wasn't sure exactly when he'd arrived, but he'd been there to see them die. Oh, how she'd wished she could have prevented that for him, but perhaps she could still do something for him.

She turned toward Tamhas and smiled. "Ye may think ye've won, but nothing ye do here will stop us."

"We shall see, as yer flesh burns." He cackled.

And he called them evil. Caitrìona pushed that thought away and focused on her goal. The fire would not be the end of them. Tamhas had to understand that, but more importantly Daniel had to hear what she had to say. So, in the distant future, he would look at their children and realize he had so much to live for.

"Light yer fire," Caitrìona dared him. "Dance in our ashes when it's done, but no matter what ye do today, we'll live on. Death isn't the end—our legacy will endure."

"What legacy?" Tamhas asked. "Is this yer way of stalling yer execution? It won't work. Ye *will* die." He snapped his fingers at the men holding torches. "Light it now." The men holding the torches lit the fire and watched as it spread through the hay and wood. It crackled as it ignited, and smoke billowed around them.

Sorcha glanced over at her and mouthed, "I'm sorry." Tears spilled down her cheeks. Her eyes were rimmed red and almost matched her fiery red hair.

Caitrìona nodded at her. "Don't fash yerself, sister dear. We'll see each other again soon." Hell wouldn't be their final resting place. They'd already lived through their own personal one. Nothing but good things were waiting for them on the other side. Caitrìona refused to believe anything else.

The flames started to lick at her feet. She sucked in a breath and breathed through the pain. They'd had so much agony already; what was a little more? She would not give in and allow Tamhas to see her as weak. Caitrìona met Tamhas's gaze, wanting him to see the determination rooted inside of her. Then she turned toward the crowd, hoping Daniel was already there. She hated that he'd see her die so horribly, but she wanted him to hear one last time how much she loved him. "My heart, the only man I've ever loved, I trust ye to ken what I'm saying. We are the *Triùir Mhòra,* and our legacy is our children. Ye can destroy our bodies, but our bloodline *will* continue on. Through them we will live."

The fire grew before them. Through the flames, she caught sight of Daniel on the edges of the crowd gathered to watch them burn. The heat no longer bothered her—she was numb to all pain and found peace in a sea of chaos. She met her husband's gaze and smiled softly. Tears flowed over his face as he blew her one last kiss. He'd understood, that's what she needed from him, then she passed out never to wake again.

ABOUT DAWN BROWER

USA TODAY Bestselling author, DAWN BROWER writes both historical and contemporary romance. There are always stories inside her head; she just never thought she could make them come to life. That creativity has finally found an outlet.

Growing up she was the only girl out of six children. She is a single mother of two teenage boys; there is never a dull moment in her life. Reading books is her favorite hobby and she loves all genres.

HISTORICAL

Stand alone:

Broken Pearl

A Wallflower's Christmas Kiss

A Gypsy's Christmas Kiss

Marsden Romances

A Flawed Jewel

A Crystal Angel

A Treasured Lily

A Sanguine Gem

A Hidden Ruby

A Discarded Pearl

Marsden Descendants

Rebellious Angel

Tempting An American Princess

How to Kiss a Debutante

Loving an America Spy

Linked Across Time

Saved by My Blackguard

Searching for My Rogue

Seduction of My Rake

Surrendering to My Spy

Spellbound by My Charmer

Stolen by My Knave

Separated from My Love

Scheming with My Duke

Secluded with My Hellion

Secrets of My Beloved

Spying on My Scoundrel

Shocked by My Vixen

Smitten with My Christmas Minx

Vision of Love

Enduring Legacy

The Legacy's Origin

Charming Her Rogue

Ever Beloved

Forever My Earl

Always My Viscount

Infinitely My Marquess

Eternally My Duke

Bluestockings Defying Rogues

When An Earl Turns Wicked

A Lady Hoyden's Secret

One Wicked Kiss

Earl In Trouble

All the Ladies Love Coventry

One Less Scandalous Earl

Confessions of a Hellion

The Vixen in Red

Lady Pear's Duke

Scandal Meets Love

Love Only Me (Amanda Mariel)

Find Me Love (Dawn Brower)

If It's Love (Amanda Mariel)

Odds of Love (Dawn Brower)

Believe In Love (Amanda Mariel)

Chance of Love (Dawn Brower)

Love and Holly (Amanda Mariel)

Love and Mistletoe (Dawn Brower

The Neverhartts

Never Defy a Vixen

Never Disregard a Wallflower

Never Dare a Hellion

Never Deceive a Bluestocking

Never Disrespect a Governess

Never Desire a Duke

CONTEMPORARY

Stand alone:

Deadly Benevolence

Snowflake Kisses

Kindred Lies

Sparkle City

Diamonds Don't Cry

Hooking a Firefly

Novak Springs

Cowgirl Fever

Dirty Proof

Unbridled Pursuit

Sensual Games

Christmas Temptation

Daring Love

Passion and Lies

Desire and Jealousy

Seduction and Betrayal

Begin Again

There You'll Be

Better as a Memory

Won't Let Go

Heart's Intent

One Heart to Give

Unveiled Hearts

Heart of the Moment

Kiss My Heart Goodbye

Heart in Waiting

Heart Lessons

A Heart Redeemed

Kismet Bay

Once Upon a Christmas

New Year Revelation

All Things Valentine

Luck At First Sight

Endless Summer Days

A Witch's Charm

All Out of Gratitude

Christmas Ever After

AFTERWORD

Thank you so much for taking the time to read my book.
Your opinion matters!
Please take a moment to review this book on your favorite review site and share your opinion with fellow readers.

www.authordawnbrower.com